SPIRITS, FAIRIES, AND MERPEOPLE

SPIRITS, FAIRIES, AND MERPEOPLE

Native Stories of Other Worlds

C.J. TAYLOR

Tundra Books

For my little friends
Zachary, Vanya, and Octavia

Text and illustrations copyright © 2009 by C.J. Taylor

Published in Canada by Tundra Books,
75 Sherbourne Street, Toronto, Ontario M5A 2P9

Published in the United States by Tundra Books of Northern New York,
P.O. Box 1030, Plattsburgh, New York 12901

Library of Congress Control Number: 2008909731

Library and Archives Canada Cataloguing in Publication

Taylor, C. J. (Carrie J.), 1952-
    Spirits, fairies, and merpeople / C.J. Taylor.

ISBN 978-0-88776-872-9

    1. Indians of North America – Folklore. 2. Water spirits. 3. Mermaids. 4. Mermen. 5. Fairies. 6. Legends – North America. 7. Indians of North America – Juvenile literature. I. Title.

PS8589.A88173S65 2009   j398.2'08997   C2008-906646-4

We acknowledge the financial support of the Government of Canada through the Book Publishing Industry Development Program (BPIDP) and that of the Government of Ontario through the Ontario Media Development Corporation's Ontario Book Initiative. We further acknowledge the support of the Canada Council for the Arts and the Ontario Arts Council for our publishing program.

ONTARIO ARTS COUNCIL
CONSEIL DES ARTS DE L'ONTARIO

Design: Kong Njo

Printed and bound in Canada

1 2 3 4 5 6   14 13 12 11 10 09

CONTENTS

THE MERMAID

✳

MI'KMAQ
The Coastal Regions of Nova Scotia

The shores of the great, gray eastern sea were home to Lone Bird. His people were the Mi'kmaq and they loved their unforgiving coast. Lone Bird knew each rock and cove and high, craggy cliff.

One day, however, when he scrambled over some rocks at the foot of a cliff, he came upon a lovely cove he had never seen before, and from that cove came the sound of splashing water. He crept closer. Soon he could hear playful laughter. He crept closer still.

Five maidens were swimming and playing in the water. They were lovely, it is true, but they looked nothing like human maidens, for humans do not have pale skin, spotted with silvery scales. They do not dress their hair with strands of seaweed. And though maidens adorn themselves with necklaces of bright shells, humans have legs. Their bodies do not end in long fish tails.

"Hello," called Lone Bird, in a voice as friendly as he could make it. He did not want to startle the maidens, but they dove under the water the instant they heard him.

Lone Bird longed to see them again. He returned the next day and found a new hiding place among the jagged rocks, and waited and waited in case they returned. Just as he was about to give up, the five water maidens appeared.

Lone Bird watched from his hiding place as they splashed in the clear pool, playing their watery games. How he longed to capture one! He jumped out from his hiding place, into the water, and swam as fast as he could. But he was not fast enough, and the maidens disappeared under the surface once again.

Lone Star did not give up. On the third day, he returned and searched for another hiding place. The water's edge was lined with tall reeds. He found a hollow one to breathe through and sank beneath the surface of the cold water. There he waited. He did not have to wait long.

When the water maidens appeared this time, they looked around cautiously but saw no danger. They began their water games as Lone Bird swam closer and closer underwater. At last, he seized one of the lovely ocean creatures.

"Let me go. Please! I have a husband and three children who wait for me back home." The frightened creature spoke sweetly, but Lone Bird did not release his grip.

The creature spoke again. "My youngest sister, Minnow, has been watching you for a long time and has fallen in love with you, but she is very shy. Let me return to my family, and I will gladly bring her to you tomorrow." Lone Bird could not deny her plea. He let her go, and she darted away through the water.

As she promised, the very next day the water maiden returned with Minnow. When Lone Bird saw the young girl, he fell madly in love, for she was the most beautiful creature he had ever seen. When she smiled at him, he knew she loved him too.

"How can we be together?" he asked. "I cannot live underwater."

"My father, Chief of All the Oceans, has granted my wish to leave him and to be with you. I will live in your village," Minnow told him. She took Lone Bird's hand and stepped ashore. To his amazement, her fish tail was transformed into feet, the webbing disappeared from her hands, and the scales fell from her skin.

Together, Minnow and Lone Bird returned to his village, where they were married. Minnow quickly learned the ways of the humans, and they soon grew to love her. The couple lived happily for many seasons.

Lone Bird thought he could not be happier until his beloved wife gave birth to a little girl they named Sea Pebble. Although Minnow was content with her life among the people of the village, she never forgot her watery home. She told Sea Pebble many stories of her sisters and her great father, Chief of All the Oceans.

"I would like to visit my aunts and grandfather," said Sea Pebble one day.

Minnow was feeling homesick herself. "Perhaps it is time to go back for a visit."

And so Lone Bird, Minnow, and Sea Pebble prepared for the journey to the underwater world that was once Minnow's home. As they approached the rocky shore and lovely cove where Lone Bird had first seen his beautiful wife, he grew afraid.

"I cannot live underwater. And what if our daughter cannot do so, either?"

"Do not worry, husband. My father has always granted me what I wish. And I wish to bring my family home." Holding his hand, their little daughter strapped securely on her back, Minnow led them slowly into the water.

Deeper and deeper they went, until they came to a great underwater village. Lone Bird was surprised to see how big and grand it was, with its many lodges and people. They were greeted by Minnow's sisters, father, and all the water people. It was a joyous time.

Minnow was happy to see her family. They shared their news and she told them of the very different world in which she now lived.

After a while, it was Lone Bird who grew homesick. He missed the blue skies, the trees, the songbirds, and all the earthly things he knew. Minnow saw her husband's sadness. "It has been a grand visit," she said, "but I think it is time to return to our earthly home."

Once again, the little family prepared for a journey, this time back to Lone Bird's village. With Sea Pebble strapped on her back and Lone Bird following close behind, the three swam upwards toward the air.

Suddenly, out of the murky depths of the cold waters a shark appeared. Minnow feared for her family. She guided Lone Bird to a large patch of seaweed. "Hide here. I am a stronger swimmer than you," she told him. "I will lead the shark away."

She strapped Sea Pebble to Lone Bird's back. "Once the shark is following me, swim as quickly as you can and don't look back. I will meet you on the shore once it is safe."

Minnow swam out of their hiding place among the fronds of seaweed. She splashed and made waves to get the shark's attention, and sure enough, the shark followed her. Lone Bird seized the moment. He swam as quickly as he could, up, up to the shore. Neither he nor the child he was carrying looked back.

Safely ashore, Lone Bird and Sea Pebble sat and waited and waited, but in his heart, Lone Bird knew he would never see Minnow again. She had given her life to save her family.

THE LITTLE PEOPLE

✳

KAHNAWAKE
The Mohawk Territory of Southern Quebec

Outside the longhouse, the wailing wind whips the snow into high drifts. Grandmother Moon peeks through the racing clouds. All the animals are safely tucked away in their dens and burrows. It is so cold that the wolf won't even be howling tonight.

Inside the longhouse, a log is thrown on the fire. Sparks shoot up and dance through the dark smoke hole to join the stars in the cold, night sky. Wisps of smoke swirl around the drying corn, beans, and squash hanging from the longhouse rafters.

The birch-bark walls are lined with baskets of ground corn and bundles of hollow reeds and painted clay pots, filled with dry meat, berries, and fish. Above the fur-lined sleeping platforms are shelves piled with soft tanned hides, baskets of shells in glowing colors, sewing awls, and lengths of sinew.

The elders sit by the warm lodge fire, quietly talking of past winters. The women are stitching and beading new moccasins, shirts, and leggings. The men dream of the spring hunt as they craft new bows and arrows. Children fidget as they wait. Finally, it is time.

The storyteller has arrived. She is a grand old woman and holds the stories of the people, the ancient ones. The longhouse grows silent, except for the crackling of the fire. The women lay aside their sewing, the men their bows, and the children stop fidgeting. Even the elders fall silent. No one is too old for a good story.

Taking her place by the fire, the storyteller begins.

Long ago, there was a village such as this. The people were fortunate in their wealth. The fine gardens gave all the corn, beans, and squash the women could dry and store. The berries were so sweet and big, it took only a few to fill a basket. The forest provided all the roots and plants for medicines and healing potions. The moose, deer, and fowl were so plentiful that the hunters rarely missed their mark. The fish swam into the nets that were laid across the streams.

Their shelters were warm and sturdy and held many fires. Everyone had gathered enough firewood to keep the longhouse cozy all winter. All was in readiness for the long, cold season to begin. The people waited peacefully.

All except four young men. They were restless and bored. "There is nothing to do," they complained, looking to Red Bird, the eldest of the group. He was the one with ideas. Some good. Some not.

"There is still plenty of game," he said. "Let's go on a hunt." The others agreed and went about collecting their bows and arrows and packing their travel bundles.

"Why are you going, Red Bird?" said his mother. "We do not need any more meat. It would only be wasted."

"We do not go for meat. We go for fun," he said as he prepared his travel bundle.

"The nights are cold. Take a warm blanket," said his mother. Red Bird knew not to argue with her and packed the fur robe she handed him.

The young men set off on the hunt. They walked and walked until Red Bird spotted the tracks of a small herd of deer in the muddy trail. They followed the tracks without taking note of their direction.

Soon the young men were lost, deep in a part of the forest they had never been before. "There is something strange about this place," said one of the youths nervously.

"It's as if the woods are watching us," said another.

The third agreed.

Red Bird did not listen. He was intent on finding the herd of deer. "I am sure we are close," he said, pointing to the tracks that led deeper into the strange, unfamiliar forest.

"But we are lost," they told him.

"Don't worry. We followed the tracks here – we can follow them back." Red Bird always had ideas. Still, it was a strange place.

Once again the young men set off, following the tracks deeper and deeper into the dark woods. Finally they came upon an overgrown meadow where the herd of deer were browsing. It was not long before their arrows flew, felling many of the animals.

"We cannot carry all this home," the young men complained.

"Take only a little meat and all the hides. We can use them in trade," Red Bird told them. They prepared several bundles of hides for travel and left the meat to rot.

When all was ready, Red Bird looked for the muddy trail that had lead them to the meadow. It was gone. He did not want to worry his friends, so

Red Bird picked another path. For days and days they wandered, lost in the strange forest. The weather grew colder. Their bundles grew heavier. The little bit of food they had was long gone. Worst of all, they felt that they were being watched.

The young men began to argue. "We should go this way," said one.

"No, no. It is this way," said another. "I am certain that the path is this way."

"You are all wrong. We must continue on this path."

Each of them pointed in a different direction.

The four young men, weak from starvation and despair, thought about the meat they had left to rot in the meadow and regretted their wastefulness.

Suddenly, a pile of dry yellow leaves rustled. A small man, the smallest they had ever seen, brushed the leaves from his tunic. "You are suffering because you have been greedy and wasteful and you killed for pleasure. I am one of the Little People. Give us your hides and you will have food."

The little man handed Red Bird a twig and a pebble. "Talk about it if you wish, and when you have decided, you may summon me with three taps on the stone." Then, he vanished as quickly as he had appeared.

"We have nothing but the hides. If they don't give us a little food, we will still starve before we get home." The others agreed.

Red Bird had an idea. "We must learn from this. We will hunt only for meat, without greed or wastefulness. In exchange for the hides, we will ask for food, certainly, but we will also ask for a guide to show us the way home." No sooner did he tap twig to pebble than the little man appeared.

"I see you have learned your lesson, so your request will be granted.

Follow me." He led them to a cave where they could wait for a guide. Before they could speak, he disappeared once again.

The young men looked around the cave. A cooking skin full of meat, beans, corn, and squash was hanging over a crackling, warm fire. They ate until they could eat no more and feel asleep.

The next morning, the four young men awoke to an astonishing sight. Each of them was wrapped in his sleeping robes, safe at home in their longhouse.

Everyone was surprised to see them for they had been gone a very long time. The young men told of their adventure in the deepest part of the forest.

"How is it that you were able to return to us?" asked one of the elders. "Few ever do."

The young men looked at one another. "It was with the help of the Little People," answered Red Bird.

THE LODGE EATER

DAKOTA
The Great Plains

Spotted Bear and Broken Feather were following a hunting trail when they heard an odd cry sounding from deep in the woods. They followed the cry and, in the underbrush beneath a big tree, they found a tiny baby wrapped in a soft fur blanket.

Spotted Bear picked up the crying baby and held it close, but it wailed all the louder.

"This is a spirit baby. We must leave it here," said Broken Feather. He was a superstitious young man.

"We cannot leave the child to starve. We will take the infant to our chief. He is a wise man and will know what to do." Spotted Bear patted the baby's back, but its wailing grew louder and louder.

When Spotted Bear and Broken Feather arrived at the village they went straight to the chief's tepee. As soon as they entered, the baby stopped its wailing and fell asleep. The chief listened to the two young men as they told of finding the little child all alone in the woods. He reached out to take the tiny infant from Spotted Bear.

As the chief held the baby in his arms, his heart softened. He called to his youngest daughter, Blue Cloud. "This child is to be your son," he told her. She looked into the infant's round, sleeping face and her heart softened, too.

"He is beautiful, Father. I will take good care of him." Blue Cloud nuzzled the baby.

The chief turned back to Spotted Bear and Broken Feather. "Tell all the people there is to be a great feast tonight in honor of my new grandson."

As the two young men went about the village inviting people to the chief's feast, Broken Feather spoke again of his fears. "There is something not right with this. It is very odd."

"You worry too much. This is a time to celebrate. Blue Cloud has a new son. Our chief is happy," Spotted Bear reassured him.

The people were overjoyed as they prepared for the feast. Great amounts of food were soon cooking over campfires around the village, filling the air with delicious aromas. The women wore their finest dresses and took special care with their hair, braiding it neatly and tying it with strings of hide and feathers. The men donned long hide shirts beautifully decorated with colorful beads and long fringes.

Everyone gathered in a circle in the center of the village. When the chief arrived with Blue Cloud and the baby, he held the child up for all to see. "This is the child that has been adopted by my daughter Blue Cloud. This celebration and feast is in his honor."

As soon as the chief sat down, the drums and singing began, softly and slowly at first, then louder and faster as the people joined the dancing. Late into the night they danced until, one by one, they returned to their lodges and fell into a deep sleep.

Only the chief's daughter remained awake. The child lay in her lap, tiny mouth ajar, sleeping peacefully. In the night stillness, she heard the distant murmur of voices. They grew louder as they grew nearer. Blue Cloud did not want to wake the sleeping baby, so she called softly to the chief. "Father, I hear people approaching. I fear it may be our enemies. You must warn the people!"

The chief threw off his sleeping robes and rushed out of the tepee. He looked around cautiously and listened carefully, but he saw nothing and heard nothing. Satisfied that all was as it should be, he returned to the lodge.

Again, Blue Cloud heard the voices. She held the baby close. It was then that she realized the voices came from the open mouth of the sleeping child. Careful not to wake him, she laid the baby on the ground. "It is the child," she whispered to her father. "The voices are coming from inside the child."

The voices grew louder and louder. "This is not a child but an evil spirit come to destroy us," the chief said softly. "We must leave before he awakes, or he will swallow the whole village."

Quickly and quietly the chief crept from the tepee to find Broken Feather and Spotted Bear. "Warn everyone! The child is an evil spirit. We must leave before he wakes. His power is greatest at night."

Spotted Bear and Broken Feather moved silently from lodge to lodge, and soon the entire village had packed and slipped away unheard. Nothing remained of the village but the evil-spirit child sleeping on the ground where the chief's tepee had been.

The next morning, as the sun rose above the horizon, the tiny child woke to find himself all alone. He flew into a terrible rage, as the evil spirit changed from his baby form into a great, ugly terrifying beast. He had become a giant with a massive head and body perched high atop tall, spindly legs, barely able to walk. From its huge mouth lined with sharp, pointy teeth, came screeching as he wobbled back and forth in search of the fleeing people.

Once the people were a safe distance away, a party of brave warriors retraced their steps with their bows, arrows, and spears. They quickly slew the great, ugly spirit. As the huge beast fell to the ground dying, an entire village – tepees and people – emerged from its gaping mouth.

"Thank you for freeing us," the people cried. "Never again need we fear the evil spirit Lodge Eater."

Water Lily Finds Her Love

*

Coos
American West Oregon Coast

Water Lily and her five older brothers lived in a village where the western sea met the land. Her brothers worried about her. Other maidens her age had husbands and children to care for. "Why do you not choose one of the fine young men from our village?" they often asked.

But Water Lily showed no interest in the young men of the village. "My love is in the ocean," she would say. Her brothers could only shake their heads and wonder. Water Lily preferred to spend all her time alone, walking beside the ever-changing ocean and swimming in the coves along the shore.

Water Lily was often gone for long periods of time, making her brothers worry even more. Once, Water Lily did not return for a very long time, indeed. For three seasons her five brothers and many other villagers searched for her. She was not to be found anywhere. People said "How sad it is that the ocean has taken her."

But one day Water Lily did return, and she was not alone. She had with her a small baby. Her brothers and all the villagers rejoiced that she was home, but they wondered about the child.

"Where did this tiny baby come from?" they asked. "Where is his father?"

"He is my son," was her only reply.

As the days passed, the baby cried day and night. Everyone in the lodge complained. "We have no peace from this constant crying." Water Lily took the baby and a willow basket and went into the woods to gather roots and berries. The baby wailed loudly all the way.

A great patch of blackberry bushes grew near the shore. The berries were juicy and sweet. Water Lily placed the crying infant at the foot of a tall tree. She began filling her basket with the berries and suddenly realized that the crying had stopped. Water Lily returned to the tall tree where she'd left the baby. She was astonished to find him contentedly gnawing on a piece of fish.

"Where did the fish come from?" She looked around. A tall, handsome young man emerged from the trees. His skin was as green as the ocean and his head was covered in flowing white sea foam. Strings of pink and coral shells hung around his neck.

"My son was hungry so I gave him food," he said.

"Who are you and where do you come from?" asked Water Lily.

"I am your husband, your love from the ocean. I have come for my family."

Water Lily picked up the baby, now happily sucking on his piece of fish, and followed the strange young man to a small cove, hidden beyond the blackberry patch. He held out a webbed hand. "Water Lily, my love. I am taking you home." She cradled the child and stepped into the dark water.

The three swam deep, deep to the bottom of the sea, where they came upon a great underwater village. And there they lived in peace and health. Water Lily never returned to her village, but she told her small son tales of his uncles' great skills. One day, the child said, "I would like to be a great hunter, like my uncles." So Water Lily made a small bow and fashioned arrows for him.

The child protested. "These arrows are not straight."

Water Lily replied, "I know. Your uncles were the arrow-makers, not I. I will visit them and bring you back straighter arrows."

Water Lily prepared for her journey. She knew that her brothers liked sea otter skins, so she prepared a bundle of five of the softest, thickest pelts. "These will be their gift in exchange for the arrows." Carrying the bundle of pelts, she swam up, up until she reached the water's surface.

Water Lily lifted her head and saw a movement on the shore. Hunters were standing on the rocks, aiming at her. She recognized them as her brothers. "Don't shoot," she cried. "It's me, Water Lily, back from the ocean!"

"You can't be Water Lily! She was taken by the ocean long ago."

Water Lily swam closer to shore. "Look, it's me!" she called.

They did look, but she was not the sister they remembered. This was a strange creature with green and scaly skin. Her hair was twined with pink seaweed strands. She held out the otter skins in her webbed hands. "It is me. I have been gone a long, long time, but my love and my family are in the ocean."

The brothers conferred. This was Water Lily, the sister they had lost. She stayed in the sea, but she told them of her family and the great underwater village that was now her home. "My son wishes to be a great hunter like you. I'd like to trade these skins for some of your fine arrows."

The brothers were pleased to see Water Lily and to hear of her contentment. They gave her many arrows to take to their nephew. Before she vanished into the depths she said, "I have one more gift for you. The people of the underwater village will send a whale to your beach tomorrow. Divide the meat among all the people and tell them that I will always remember them."

The five brothers never saw Water Lily again, but their earth village received many gifts of whale meat. And in return, they would shoot their arrows into the ocean, gifts for the people under the sea.

The Fairy Village

✳

Ojibwa
Woodlands and Central North America

Long ago, among the Ojibwa there was an important chief, and that chief had ten daughters. The daughters all married men who were good hunters and strong, courageous warriors. All except Red Leaf, that is.

Red Leaf fell in love with Star Talker and though her sisters objected, she married him. He was old and feeble. He was so frail that he could barely walk. But whenever anyone wondered aloud about the match, Red Leaf would say, "I love him and I am happy."

One evening the ten sisters and their husbands and all their many children were invited to come to their father's lodge for a great feast. As they made their way there, Star Talker stopped many times to rest and to speak to the stars.

"Look! He thinks Evening Star is his father," said one of the sisters.

They continued on their way and came upon a hollow log lying beside the trail. Star Talker dropped to his knees and crawled through one end. When he came out the other, he was no longer old and feeble. He had changed into a handsome young man. His white hair was a shiny long mane. He stood straight and tall. But Red Leaf had changed too.

No longer was she a beautiful young woman. She was frail and old. Her lovely black hair had become stringy and gray. Her back was bent, her smooth skin now dry and wrinkled. But this did not change the love they had for each other.

When they arrived at the chief's lodge, a voice came from the heavens. It was Evening Star. "I have come to speak with my son, Star Talker. Long ago an evil star cast a spell that turned you into an old man wandering the earth. Because of the love you and your wife, Red Leaf, share, the spell has been broken. You are free to return home, and you may bring Red Leaf and all her family to live among the stars."

Suddenly the ten sisters, their husbands, all their many children, and their father, the chief, floated upwards, changing into birds with bright-colored feathers. Evening Star placed the birds in a cage atop the clouds.

Again Evening Star's voice rang out from the heavens. This time, his words were a warning to Star Talker. "Take care not to stand in the light of the evil star or the spell will return."

All lived happily in the heavens for many years, Evening Star happiest of all, for his son Star Talker and Star Talker's earthly wife, Red Leaf, gave him a grandson named Flicker. Evening Star loved the little boy very much and could deny him nothing. The two spent their time watching the world below and all the people who lived there.

Flicker particularly loved to watch the young men hunting. "I would like to be a great hunter someday, like the people." So Evening Star fashioned a little bow and arrows for his grandson.

"You must practice every day if you wish to be a great hunter," said Evening Star.

For many days Flicker shot his arrows into the clouds. His aim got better and better. One day he told his grandfather, "I cannot be a great hunter if I have only clouds to shoot." Evening Star could not refuse a wish from his grandson. He opened the cage atop the clouds.

All the beautifully colored birds flew out of the open door. Flicker took careful aim and shot one arrow, then another. The third arrow flew from his bow and met its mark. It pierced the breast of a robin.

Flicker was proud and wanted to show his grandfather. But before he could pick up the tiny bird it changed back into its earthly form. Flicker felt himself floating down through the heavens until at last his feet touched the earth. All the colorful birds that had flown among the heavenly clouds began to drift back to earth. As they came closer, they changed back into their human forms. But they were no bigger than pine cones.

The tiny people came to rest atop the mossy cliffs that stood high above a rushing waterfall. There they built their lodges of flower stems and wore robes of flower petals. They were happy to be back in their earthly world. They thanked Evening Star for giving them a beautiful new home.

Today, if we listen very hard, we can still hear the tiny people singing and dancing and giving thanks in the soft light of the Evening Star.

SPIRITS OF HEAVEN AND EARTH

✴

UTE
The Plains of Utah and Colorado

In the beginning, when the universe was young, there were two heavens. The farther heaven of planets, moon, and stars was the dwelling place of the higher spirits. Below was the other heaven, where the lesser spirits had created the earth with its mountains, plains, seas and rivers, and all the living things upon it.

The finest creation in Lower Heaven was corn. When the lesser spirits made corn, they were satisfied with what they had done. "Our corn needs care," they said, and made people to tend to it.

The people needed food and water and shelter so they could live and tend the corn. So the spirits gave them clean rushing rivers, game to hunt for food, and shelter. All of this was so they could tend the corn.

The people had everything they needed to live in contentment, but they were stiff-necked. They argued and fought amongst themselves.

"We have given them everything they need to live in peace and yet they carp and bicker," said the lesser spirits. "We cannot let this continue."

So the lesser spirits gathered up woven baskets, the largest they could find. They placed gold and silver in some of them, the richest earth in others. And, of course, they filled others with corn. When they knew that they had preserved all of the earth's treasures they caused the waters to rise.

The flood drowned the forests and plains. It swept away all living things. And it washed the earth of the ungrateful people.

The lesser spirits took their baskets of gold and silver and of fertile earth and of corn, and left the lower heaven to join the higher spirits. But when they were above the clouds the higher spirits stopped them. "There is no way into heaven with the things you carry," they said.

The lesser spirits had no choice. Hearts breaking, they emptied their baskets into the sky. The gold and silver and rich soil fell and fell back to the earth into mounds that stood above the swirling waters. The last baskets they emptied contained precious corn. It landed on the mounds of gold and silver and earth. But some of the lesser spirits could not bear to part with all of the corn. They hid some away. It was only a little, they told themselves.

Sometimes the lesser spirits would eat of the secret corn, but on the whole, they lived happily in the far heaven. One day, as they were looking down on the mounds of gold and silver and dark earth, they saw a young man and woman.

"They must have survived the rising of the waters," said one spirit. The spirits watched as the people planted tiny seeds of corn in the rich dark earth. And they watched the couple tending the shoots as they grew. Their care for the corn touched the lesser spirits. "We will not despair of them. We will give them another chance," they said.

So the lesser spirits called up to the rain clouds, the home of the Great Lizard. Now, the Great Lizard had a thirst that could not be quenched. They told him of the flooded world below and all the water there.

Great Lizard slithered out of the rain clouds and down to earth. He lowered his head to the waters and began to drink. He drank and he drank and the waters fell. And as the waters fell, the earth rose.

Soon Great Lizard had drunk the earth dry and was ready to return to the rain clouds. But his body was too bloated with water. He flew for a moment and then crashed back to earth. When he landed he turned to stone that shattered. And from his shattered body poured streams and rivers that fed the dry soil.

Once again the earth was a good place for people to live. The lesser spirits kept watch from up in the heavens, every now and then tasting from their hidden cache of corn. Sometimes a kernel falls, and we see a shooting star.

Souls in the Mist

❋

CREE
Plains and Woodlands of Canada and Northern U.S.A.

The universe was ruled by two spirits. The Great Spirit ruled the heavens and the earth and all that was good. Evil Minded ruled the underworld and all that was wicked. At the beginning of time they came to an agreement. When the people died, the souls of those who had lived with love, respect, and kindness would spend eternity shining in the heavens with the Great Spirit. The souls of those who had done wrong would go to the underworld to be tormented eternally by Evil Minded.

This arrangement worked out well, for there were as many evil souls as good souls to be collected; that is, until Three Crow.

Three Crow was an ancient wise man who lived among the Cree. He loved and honored the Great Spirit. Because of his love and devotion, the Great Spirit gave Three Crow a wonderful gift. He was given the knowledge of healing plants and roots and the understanding to use them.

Whether Three Crow was called upon for a healing potion, or whether he was asked for advice, all the people knew they could depend on him. He taught the people to follow the path of love, respect, and kindness. "And in doing so," he would tell them, "you will be welcomed by the Great Spirit in the heavens." He warned them about Evil Minded and his terrible underworld. "His is a path to eternal torment and torture."

Evil Minded hated Three Crow. Because of his teachings, there were fewer wrong-doing souls and fewer souls to torture. Evil Minded tried many ways to tempt people into wrong doing. He promised them wealth and power, but only a few chose the path to the underworld.

Evil Minded went to the Great Spirit. "We had an agreement," he raged, his voice thundering through the heavens. "You had as many good souls as I had bad, and I had as many bad as you had good. Because of Three Crow, my world is almost empty!"

"Three Crow has taught the people to live with love and respect," replied the Great Spirit. "When they come to me they are good."

"But no one is good all the time," argued Evil Minded. "Even the best do bad things sometimes."

"This is true. We will make a new agreement." Great Spirit thought for some time before he spoke again. "I will give you all the souls for three days and nights. In that time we will see those with true love in their hearts. I will welcome them into my heavens. You may keep the rest."

Evil Minded happily agreed, but before he could rush off to kindle his welcoming fires, the Great Spirit added another condition to the agreement. "You must promise to burn your fires only in the marshy lowlands. We do not want you to set the whole world on fire."

"Yes, yes, I promise," Evil Minded called out as he hurried away to gather wood for his fires.

When Three Crow heard of the new agreement, he grew sick at heart and grieved for the people. In despair, he cried out to the Great Spirit, "Please have mercy on the souls of the good. Evil Minded is cruel, and he will torture all the souls for three days and three nights. They will suffer terribly."

The Great Spirit heard Three Crow's pleas. "You are a good man and think only of the people. I will lessen their punishment. When the people die, I will give them a form Evil Minded cannot harm."

With that, Three Crow saw all the souls turn into swirling mists, mists that clung to the lowlands for three days as they waited without harm to make their journey to the heavens and the Great Spirit – or to Evil Minded and the underworld.

AFTERWORD

This gathering of mystical creatures and powerful spirits has been stirred into a magical brew. It is flavored by the love between humans and merpeople, as described in the west-coast Coos legend of Water Lily and the east-coast Mi'kmaq story, "The Mermaid." The attraction between beings of this world and others is also evident in the Ojibwa tale, "The Fairy Village."

The Cree sweeten the mixture with their version of the eternal struggle between the powers of good and evil, so common to many cultures. The Ute "Spirits of Heaven and Earth" tints the concoction with images of the land's riches and shooting stars. The Mohawk storytellers of Kahnawake contribute a pinch of greed, wastefulness, and forgiveness to the mix, while the Dakota add robust flavor with a wise chief and his brave warriors.

I hope you have drunk deeply and enjoyed every ingredient of this elixir, for it contains the tang of seawater, the pungent warmth of the soil, the refreshing mists of the sky, and the sweet voices of storytellers from a time gone by. *Nia wen*. Thank you.

C.J. Taylor